To Pops, the best dad in the universe
—TL

For Anthony, to whom all dogs are alien
—MB

Bloop
Text copyright © 2021 by Tara Lazar
Illustrations copyright © 2021 by Mike Boldt

ISBN 978-0-06-287160-2

The artist used Painter and Photoshop to create the digital illustrations for this book.
Typography by Rachel Zegar
21 22 23 24 25 RTLO 10 9 8 7 6 5 4 3 2 1
❖
First Edition

BLOOP

WRITTEN BY
TARA LAZAR

ILLUSTRATED BY
MIKE BOLDT

HARPER
An Imprint of HarperCollinsPublishers

Training to be the next ruler of Planet XYZ was hard work. Bloop tried to follow all the emperor's rules, regulations, and robots.

But . . .

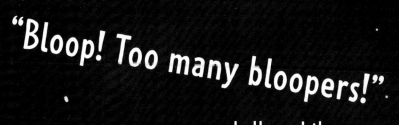

"Bloop! Too many bloopers!"
bellowed the emperor.

Disappointed with Bloop's progress, the emperor issued a decree: Bloop had one week to conquer Earth and prove himself a worthy leader. "If you can rule that crazy planet, then you can rule XYZ!"

When Bloop landed on Earth, he instantly knew who was in charge.

Large creatures carried, chased, and scooped. They must be serving the superior fluff balls.

WOOF! said one hairy creature.

"Take me to your leader!"

BARK! said the next.

GRRR! The third just growled and refused to speak.

Hmm . . . Bloop's takeover of Earth might take longer than expected.

Bloop staked out a spot to spy on these spunky creatures.
He learned all their secrets.

How they acquired
their super speed . . .

how they inspected their empire . . .

and where they stored their priceless treasures.

Aha! To be ruler, maybe Bloop had to collect treasures!

He stockpiled their most valuable belongings. They had to bow down to Bloop now!

Instead, they just BOW-WOW-WOWed.

These were clever creatures indeed!
They were everywhere—and so was their paralyzing interstellar slime!

Time was running out. Bloop summoned the emperor for advice.

The emperor's hologram bellowed,

"Bloop! Too many bloopers!"

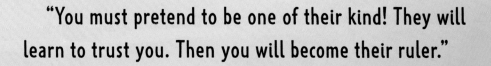

"You must pretend to be one of their kind! They will learn to trust you. Then you will become their ruler."

Bloop tried hard to blend in. He got down on all fours
and he tucked in his floofers.

He chased the commoners.

He finally took revenge on robots.

He bounded through neighborhoods, parks, and fields.
Bloop had never known such fun, such freedom!

And then he dashed right into . . .

the royal guard!

The guard chauffeured Bloop to an exclusive royal retreat.

They must have recognized Bloop's greatness! Now it wouldn't be long until he became ruler.

Bloop had plenty of gourmet nourishment and squishy, squeaky gizmos.
He realized these were for calling the servants.
A small, sticky one approached.

"Oh. Mommy, him, him, him, PUHLEEZE?!"

"Let's see . . . must be a rare breed," said the lady-in-waiting. "Yes, let's take him!"

They hugged Bloop
so tightly, his floofers
popped out.

When Bloop arrived at his new accommodations, he instantly knew who was in charge . . . HE WAS!

Bloop's servants provided for his every need.
When his floofers itched, they knew just what to do.
They bestowed on him the crown jewels.

And his new palace was fit for an emperor.

When Bloop's servants took him to survey his
kingdom, all his loyal subjects bowed down.

Bloop had done it. He had conquered Earth! He was the supreme leader!

The emperor summoned Bloop.
"Mission accomplished, Bloop. Return to Planet XYZ ASAP.
Your kingdom awaits."

Bloop had a tough time packing
his treasures. The royal footman kept
throwing them far, far away. But Bloop
liked the chase . . .

and afterward, he relished the rewards.

This planet dazzled Bloop! Earth boasted fantastic riches, including something called "bacon."

What a way to live!

But Bloop knew it was time to return to his planet. He had to say goodbye.

Then the teeniest-tiniest servant spoke.

"I love you."

Bloop glowed.

Bloop had never seen a planet as exciting as Earth . . .
and he had never known a feeling as wonderful as this.

Bloop sent the emperor a transmission.

"Bloop sit.

Bloop **STAY**."

Yes, life on Earth was going swell for Bloop.
He had found his true home . . . and a new mission:

Defending his throne from
an alien invader!